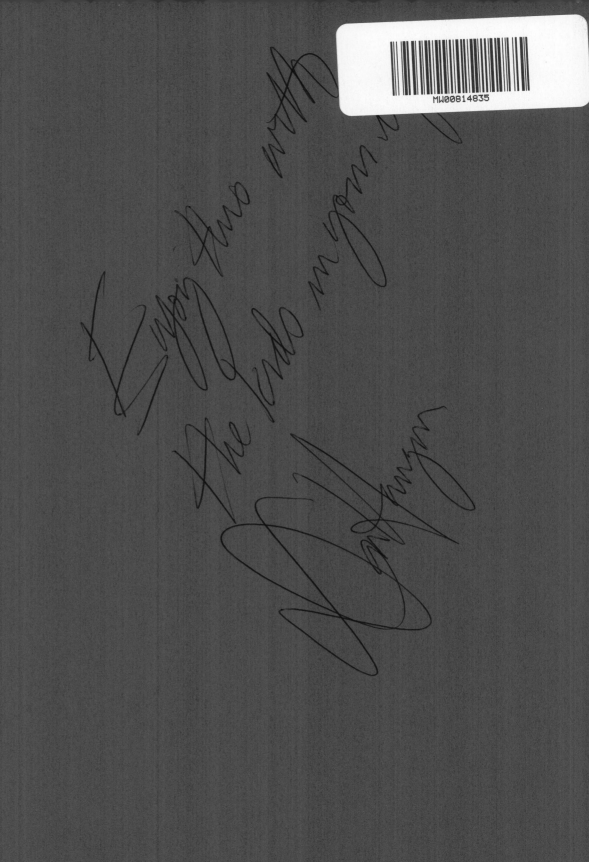

Staarabu was Wise, Anana was Gentle

by Dan Haugen with Illustrations by Shawn McCann

Illustrated by Shawn McCann • Visit: www.ShawnMcCann.com

Proceeds from the sale of STAARABU WAS WISE, ANANA WAS GENTLE will benefit Simpson Housing Services, a homeless shelter in Minneapolis, Minnesota.

ISBN 10: 1-59298-335-9
ISBN 13: 978-1-59298-335-3

Library of Congress Catalog Number: 2010926525

Printed in the United States of America
First Printing: 2010

14 13 12 11 10   5 4 3 2 1

Cover and interior typesetting by James Monroe Design, LLC.

Beaver's Pond Press, Inc.
7104 Ohms Lane, Suite 101
Edina, MN 55439-2129
(952) 829-8818
www.BeaversPondPress.com

To order, visit www.BeaversPondBooks.com
or call (800) 901-3480. Reseller discounts available.

For all those looking for a home,
and for my parents who have now gone home.

Many of us feel that we are incapable of making the changes needed in our world. We fear that our resources (influence, money, ideas, and time) are too little to matter. Dan Haugen's beautifully crafted story portrays how a tiny mouse and his elephant friend discover that together they have the courage to act. The results are life changing. This genuine call to do what we are capable of is one that each of us can take to heart and make real in our own communities.

Profits from sales of this book will be dedicated to a homeless shelter in Minneapolis, Minnesota by the name of Simpson Housing Services (www.simpsonhousing.org). Dan Haugen walks his talk and reminds us that we each have the power to make a positive change in our world. I commend *Staarabu was Wise, Anana was Gentle* to readers of all ages.

—Julie Manworren—
Executive Director
Simpson Housing Services, Inc.

Staarabu the mouse had an underground house
on *Upeo*, a vast Kenyan plain.
But with space overflowing, his large family kept growing
with more mice than his house could contain.

*To encourage dialogue between reader and child, enlarged words are explained
in the glossary at the end of this book.

And just down the savannah, lived an elephant: *Anana*.
Yes, in *Kenya*, the elephants *abound*.
Nana's herd was large, too—a wrinkled, *thunderous* crew
—unlike Bu, though, Nana lived above ground.

Despite her wide *girth*, kind Anana, since birth
was best friends with tiny Staarabu.
And she loved her playmate. Who'd have guessed their strange fate
would soon find these two saving Upeo?

Now, Staarabu means "wise," and Anana means "gentle":
special names in their native *Swahili*.
And these two friends, you'll see—yes, you'll quickly agree
—shared their wisdom and gentleness freely.

In this wide, open place, there was plenty of space.
Yes, and even the mice would agree
that the problem, I think, there was nothing to drink,
forcing most of the thirsty to *flee*.

It wasn't always this way. The elders would say
that rains once fell from June through September.
But the plain was now dry, and the brilliant blue sky
had been cloudless since all could remember.

Now, all creatures know when the *watering holes* grow
that it's easy to all get along.
It's when watering holes shrink, and there's not much to drink,
that their *trust levels* aren't quite as strong.

Such was the state on Upeo of late.
Without rain there was now *widespread drought*.
And the heat and the dust and the growing *distrust*
left the animals' futures in doubt.

They were thirsty, in pain, and with no hope of rain,
the blowing sand cut like a knife.
And the *Endurance* River was now just a sliver,
just a slow, precious trickle of life.

Slowly baked by the sun, nearly just a dry run,
the great river was barely wet sand.
And the animals worried; in fact, more and more hurried
to find more *hospitable* land.

In sheer *desperation*, the whole animal nation,
trudging slowly across the great plain,
had a shared *destination*—a brand new location—
with cool water, good food, and soft rain.

Now here comes the part—the part about heart—
when Staarabu and Nana would lead.
Though they seldom left home, and they weren't prone to roam,
they would answer their families' need.

See, their families were *shattered*, and their herds had all scattered.
They were trudging along, skin and bones.
But despite their *self-doubt*, Bu and Nana set out
all alone—not quite grown—on their own.

And the two friends were scared; they just weren't quite prepared
for a life on the *parched*, burning plain.
Their whole world had changed, and Upeo now seemed strange.
It was all very hard to explain.

Bu and Nana had fears as they fought back their tears,
but they managed to stay in control.
For the sake of their *kin*, they just would not give in,
and decided to play a brave role.

Yes, the two friends were frightened, but their attitudes brightened
as they busily hatched a bold plan.
They would head to the north; they would start to move forth
to the place where the river began.

Because problems, of course, can be traced to their source,
for the source is where problems get started.
And what's going wrong there causes trouble *elsewhere*.
Knowing that, the two bravely *departed*.

Man, it appeared, had at times interfered
with the flow of the Endurance River.
Yes, in animal *lore*, this had happened before,
leaving only a crooked, brown sliver.

So the two ventured forth, on their path to the north,
heading straight toward the village of Man.
And their fearfulness mounted, as the two scared friends counted
all the signs of Man's dangerous *clan*.

They were traveling by night, bathed in milky moonlight,
staying carefully hidden by day.
And they never were spotted, as they quietly trotted,
slyly keeping the Man clan at bay.

With Staarabu on top, and Anana below,
the two friends were now in high gear.
Then, with the sun slowly rising, they saw something surprising!
Now the source of their problem was clear.

It was almost daybreak when they came to a lake,
a lake that continued to grow.
It had grown from a dam—yes, a man-made logjam
—that was blocking Endurance's flow.

Tiny mice have sharp teeth, and it was time to *unsheathe*
little feisty Staarabu's *incisors*.
So Nana let him right down from the top of her crown.
Man would soon see that Bu was the wiser.

This dam held by ropes would not *dash* the high hopes
of the animals back on the plain.
So Staarabu just gnawed, then he scratched and he clawed,
and the lake slowly started to drain.

As the logs and ropes parted, mighty Nana got started.
She just lowered her head and pushed hard.
As the dam started creaking—as the logjam was leaking—
gentle Nana showed *calm disregard*.

And at noon that great day, the dam finally gave way,
with Staarabu and Anana *victorious*.
They were both tired and cold; but what a sight to behold!
The Endurance was once again glorious.

As the Man clan looked on at this bravery and *brawn*,
they now knew that their dam was unwise.
Yes, they'd made a mistake in creating their lake,
nearly causing the great plain's *demise*.

Man and beast stepped aside, as the river grew wide,
and a wonderful thing happened then.
Gentle Nana roared loudly; wise Staarabu beamed proudly.
In *harmony* with man once again.

And way back on the plain, joy was hard to contain,
as the news of Endurance spread fast.
All the herds had decided, as their *panic subsided*,
to return to Upeo at last.

As they took to the trail, neither timid nor frail,
Bu and Nana now knew they belonged.
They had felt unprepared, but faced danger, though scared,
and they soon found their courage was strong.

When they got to the plain, they saw fresh green *terrain*
all awash with broad smiles and good cheer.
And the herds had **ordained** that the two friends would **reign**
as brave legends who'd stood up to fear.

Whether you're big like a tree, or small like a flea,
you're just as important; its true.
See, we each play a role, *vital* parts of the whole.
That's the truth, and it's true for you, too.

And one thing is clear, when we're scared and feel fear,
that our courage is not based on size.
When it's time to stand tall, why even the small
are so often full of surprise.

Elsewhere: Another place.

Flee: To run away.

Girth: The distance around something, like the distance around an elephant's waist.

Harmony: When things fit together well, like when living things cooperate and work together.

Hospitable: Friendly and inviting.

Incisors: Very sharp teeth.

Kenya: A country in Africa.

Kin: People in your family.

Lore: Stories.

Ordained: to identify a leader, like when the animals decided Staarabu and Anana would be their new leaders.

Panic: To be really scared and not know what to do.

Parched: Very dry.

Reign: To be in charge of something or some place.

Savannah: A flat, grassy area in Africa.

Self-doubt: Not having confidence in yourself.

Shattered: Broken into pieces.

Staarabu: A Swahili word or name meaning wise.

Subsided: To become smaller, like when the level of a lake becomes lower.

Swahili: The name of a tribe of people in Africa- who also speak a language called Swahili.

Terrain: A type of land, like grassy or flat land.

Thunderous: Loud, like thunder.

Trust levels: The amount of confidence you have in someone or something.

Unsheathe: to get ready to use something sharp.

Upeo: A Swahili word or name meaning big or vast.

Victorious: Having won something.

Vital: Very important.

Watering holes: Places where animals drink.

Widespread drought: When a large area does not have enough water.